AF726965

FRANKIE

THE KING OF SIAM

FRANKIE

The King Of Siam

GEORGE H. TSEGELETOS

ReadersMagnet, LLC

Frankie: The King of Siam
Copyright © 2021 by George H. Tsegeletos. All rights reserved.

Published in the United States of America
ISBN Paperback: 978-1-955603-38-6
ISBN Hardback: 978-1-956780-12-3
ISBN eBook: 978-1-955603-37-9

All rights reserved. No part of this publication may be reproduced, stored in a retrieval system or transmitted in any way by any means, electronic, mechanical, photocopy, recording or otherwise without the prior permission of the author except as provided by USA copyright law.

The opinions expressed by the author are not necessarily those of ReadersMagnet, LLC.

ReadersMagnet, LLC
10620 Treena Street, Suite 230 | San Diego, California, 92131 USA
1.619.354.2643 | www.readersmagnet.com

Book design copyright © 2021 by ReadersMagnet, LLC. All rights reserved.
Cover design by Ericka Obando
Interior design by Mary Mae Romero

To my daughter,
Cori

Frankie with long tail

CHAPTER ONE

THE HOME COMING

It was a cold late November day as my wife Charlotte and I sat looking out our front window. We were anxiously waiting for the arrival of our son, Charles. He was returning home after having been away for several years, working at a winery in the foothills of California.

"There he is" we shouted, as we saw him pulling into our driveway in his old station wagon. Before he could even turn off the engine, his mother and I rushed out of the house and were standing next to the car to greet him.

His car was a sight, the rack on the roof was piled high with furniture, the inside was full with boxes, clothes, and everything he owned. He had just barely enough room to squeeze into the driver's seat of the car. The back of the station wagon was full, the back seat was full and even the passenger seat was full.

He stepped out, looking tired from the long drive, but otherwise he looked very healthy and happy to be home. Charles, who greeted us by talking excitedly, hadn't changed a bit. He had always been a happy child.

His mother said, "Come on in and have something to eat, we can unload the car later." It was then we heard a weird high pitched whining sound coming from within his car. "What's that noise?" we asked. "Oh" he exclaimed, "that's Frankie, my kitty. He doesn't meow like a normal cat." He went on to say that friends who were also leaving the area couldn't take the kitty where they were moving to. They had to find a new home and asked him if he could care for the kitten. Charles explained, "The weather was too cold for this kitty in the mountains. You see, this kitten is one of the shorthair types of his breed and just wouldn't be able to adjust to the cold weather in the mountains." My friends asked if I could take him with me, saying it would be much better for it to live down here in the warmer climate of my home. They gave me all his pedigree papers and his medical records and told me he was a real pure bred cat, a feline breed originally having come from the Orient. Half-heartedly we said, "Okay, bring the cat into the house and we will find something to feed him as well."

Charles then reached into a pile of clothes in the back seat of the wagon and pulled the cat out of the car. We both shouted, "It's a Siamese!" We continued to blurt out a string of questions, "It's a small kitten, how old is it, how come it has such a long tail, kind of a skinny kitten huh, what did you say his name was?" Charles answered, "His name is Frankie and he has very blue eyes, so they named him after a famous singer. I'm hungry. Let's go inside and I will tell you all I know about this wonderful kitty."

As we walked into the house, there was one question we had all forgotten to ask. Does the kitten get along with dogs? How would our black Cocker Spaniel, Chico, act when confronted by the arrival of the new family member? When we entered the house we could see down the hallway. Chico's head peeked out from one of the bedroom doors.

Looking down the hallway at us, Chico began to walk towards us. Charlie set Frankie down. Chico continued walking slowly down the hall heading straight for the little kitten. When only a foot away from Frankie, Chico stopped and then slowly took a short step closer, just close enough to where he could stretch his neck out to sniff this new family member. In a flash, Frankie leaped into the air and landed on top of Chico. With a couple of quick slaps to Chico's head, Frankie established that he was the new ruler of the house. It happened so fast we couldn't react. A slight yelp escaped from Chico and then they both walked slowly off in different directions. No scratches, no blood, no hair missing, this first meeting caused damage only to Chico's pride. In time, they would end up being the best of friends. In fact, Frankie became Chico's protector, not letting any other animal come close or bother his doggie friend.

Well, that is the story of how Frankie came to live with our family. It was the beginning of a long relationship, with many adventures, exciting moments, funny stories and long furry tales.

After his encounter with Chico, Frankie continued to go from room to room, exploring each one. After checking the whole house, he came back to the kitchen and finally settled down to eat.

Frankie was a little kitty, but boy could he eat. He could eat more food than two big cats. "Wow, he sure eats a lot for such a skinny thing," I remarked.

After eating, Frankie went into the laundry room, climbed into the laundry basket and went to sleep. Charles quickly explained, "That is where he slept in my cabin in the Foothills. It was the only place he could keep warm." Charlotte then piped in, "Well, later, we're going to the pet shop to get him a plush kitty bed fit for a King."

Frankie sitting on bed with rabbit's foot chain hanging from his mouth

CHAPTER TWO

THE RETRIEVER

Early on, we found out that one of Frankie's favorite games was retrieving. It started one day when I accidently dropped my keys with a rabbit's foot chain attached and Frankie quickly pounced on it. He began to slap it around, pick it up and throw it into the air. I took it away from him, removed the key that was on it and threw the rabbit foot across the room. He attacked with a vengeance. Everyone in the family would play the game, throwing it to every corner of the house and Frankie would retrieve it. When he finally tired of playing we would put it in his toy basket. When he was ready to play again, Frankie would go to his toy basket and take it out and bring it to one us then meow wanting the retrieving game to start again. When we didn't throw the rabbit's foot, he would make a real fuss by meowing loudly. Then if we ignored him totally and no one would throw it, he would walk away and play with it by himself. Many times in the morning while lazily lying in bed before getting up, Frankie would get his rabbit's foot, jump on the bed, and drop it on one of our heads as we lay there. I guess that was his way of telling us to not be so lazy. It was time to get up and play.

CHAPTER THREE

STRANGE BEHAVIOR

Frankie was adjusting pretty fast to his new home. However, as a precaution during this first week, we kept him confined to the inside of the house until we were sure he would not wander off and get lost. We planned to keep him locked in the house until we had felt he got used to his surroundings and learned that this was his home.

One day, he was exploring an open cabinet in the kitchen and we inadvertently shut the door locking him in it. We looked everywhere for him. We thought maybe he finally escaped. It was not long when we heard the weird meowing he always made when he wanted something. Following the sounds to the kitchen, then to the cabinet, we opened the door. Sure enough, sitting in there was Frankie. You would think he would be happy to be let out. But no, he was mad at us for locking him in!He stepped out and just strutted away, paying no attention to us, just meowing as he went on his way.

On another day, when I had gone in to take a shower, I had placed all my clean clothes on the bed and a pair of white athletic socks on my shoes. Later, while dressing, I went to put my socks and shoes on and noticed one of the socks was on the floor a few feet away! That's weird! Picking up the sock, I noticed it had a big hole. I scratched my head trying to remember why I had such a large hole in my sock and why it was put away like that. That evening while we were all eating at the dinner table, I told the hole in my sock story and added my instructions; do not put socks or other torn clothes away without repairing the item first. Of course, everyone thought I had lost my mind by even bringing up the subject; nevertheless, it didn't stop me from continuing to tell the sock story. Could the hole in my sock have gotten there in the wash or drying cycle, I asked? No comments! I thought to myself, getting the answer to this mystery would require a little more investigation. Talking to myself, I quipped if Sherlock Holmes were here, he could get to the bottom of this mystery.

The next day, Charlotte was in the bedroom and I was in the kitchen when I heard her yell out, "George, we have moths!" I hurriedly rushed to the bedroom to see what this commotion about moths was all about.

"Where are the moths?" I yelled back as I was rushing to the bedroom. "I don't know, but they are big ones. Look at the hole in my new wool sweater," she said angrily. "Wow, that can't be a moth. It would have to have jaws like a lion," I said. This was not only a real mystery, but a problem as well -- first, my socks with big holes and now, Charlotte's sweater.

The next day, the mystery was solved without any furtherinvestigating done on our part. I had just fed Frankie his breakfast in the laundry room and left to do some other chores. When I returned a short time later to pick up his dish to clean it, there was Frankie next to his dish, chewing on one of my white athletic socks. I called Char and we watched him, eat a little food then go to the sock and chew on it, then back again to the food and back to the sock. "Goodness," we said "it looks like he is cleaning his teeth after he eats some food."

We were told that since birth, Frankie had always been fed only canned food and was never fed any kibble. That explains why he chewed on the socks, just to clean his teeth. That night, we asked Charles what he knew about Frankie's chewing habit. Charles explained, "Oh yes, that's the other reason my friend gave him to me." Charles went on to say, "My friend took him to an animal physiatrist to find out about Frankie's chewing-socks and loud-meowing habit. You can see in Frankie's papers the report where the psychiatrist states his findings and answers", finished Charles. By this time I was talking to myself, Oh that's great I have a crazy cat but at least, now I know why they gave Frankie away. However, after researching the subject, we found out it is not an uncommon behavioral trait of Siamese cats. Cleaning their teeth by chewing on something made out of a natural fiber was normal. Well, I guess maybe Frankie isn't cuckoo after all.

The next day I went to the sport shop and bought a dozen white cotton athletic socks for Frankie. We were hoping this was the answer and would keep him from chewing our clothes. It worked! Problem fixed. But he sure needed a lot of socks.

We needed to get the word out to all our family members and friends how urgent it was to help us out at this time of need. An immediate response was needed! Having to support our new family member with his strange behavior and addiction, we asked everyone to please donate to our cause any old sock they might have lying around. Shortly after, donations began to pour in and continued for years; friends and relatives brought us their old white cotton socks!

Frankie carrying sweatshirt on top of fence

CHAPTER FOUR

THE CAT BURGLAR

Another year had passed since Frankie had joined our family and he never ceased to amaze us. One summer evening while we were all sitting at the kitchen table eating dinner, our daughter, Cori, happened to glance out the window and observed Frankie climbing over from the neighbor's fence then jumping down onto our patio. "You are not going to believe what I just saw. Frankie just came over the fence dragging what looked like a large sweat shirt," she said. Laughing in disbelief I asked, "You saw our Frankie bringing home a sweater that is probably three times longer than he is? Now that would be quite a feat." In moments, we all could not believe our eyes. There on the patio coming towards the kitchen door was Frankie and he was dragging a large grey sweatshirt clenched in his mouth. Jokingly, I said "We have a thief in the family!

Frankie is stealing clothes off the neighbor's clothesline -- a real cat burglar!"

In the weeks that followed, he began to amass quite a haul, with his favorite loot from the neighboring clotheslines being socks, but there were times when he would manage to drag large pieces of clothing home. One would think he would be satisfied with the socks we gave him. But no, he wanted to make sure he had enough supplies stored for his chewing habit. He was an addict and a cat burglar. It became a constant chore trying to return his loot by calling up the neighbors and trying to locate the owners.

Fight with Black Cat

CHAPTER FIVE

THE KING ESTABLISHES HIS KINGDOM

As time passed, it became obvious that Frankie was trying to establish a territory he could claim as HIS KINGDOM. He was always marking his territory by walking around our fence line, leaving his mark on everything inside the fence and thus letting all intruders know that this was his territory. In addition, Frankie started to patrol the fence line everyday to make sure no one crossed over into his Realm. Some creatures he considered his subjects and allowed within his boundary, like the lizards, birds, and people, but no cats. Once, a bunny came into his Kingdom and then a snake, but that's another story. Lizards would lose their tails on occasion, birds might lose a feather or two, and people could always expect to be swatted when walking by the crouching King. Frankie never really hurt any of his subjects that lived within his realm, but he did rough them up on occasion, I guess, just to let them know that he was King. Once in a while, he would carry in his mouth a lizard or a bird he caught back to the house. He would then gently place his catch at the feet of his people subjects, unhurt.

Now, any cat encountered within his boundary was a totally different story with Frankie. He did not get along with cats that trespassed. He considered them his enemy and would not allow them on or near his land.

One early evening, he left the house after supper and began his slow rounds patrolling around the fence line. When it became too dark, we could no longer see Frankie patrolling, but knew he would end his patrol and come home soon. It was but a short time later that we heard the vicious cat battle start. We could hear loud screeching, hissing, meowing, and roaring from two cats fighting. It was coming from the fence line on the uphill side of the house where the yard dropped steeply from the fence to the patio. I switched on the patio flood lights and there rolling down the hill with all the leaves, twigs, dirt flying, and this screeching noise, two cats with all four of their legs wrapped around each other! They were rolling down like a fur ball. I never ever heard such a loud commotion coming from two creatures fighting. It sounded like a dozen cats, not just two. When they finally landed on the patio, they came apart and just stopped and stared at each other, not making even a quiet meow. The strange cat, a big black one with yellow eyes and one white paw limped away, then quickly jumped over the fence and disappeared into the darkness. Frankie's tail looked like a big bottlebrush, his short fur stood up in lots of places with leaves and sticks poking out. He walked into the house with his head held high as if to say, there I showed that stranger who dared to trespass on the lands of my Realm.

A few days later, Frankie's face was swollen and one eye was completely shut. He had a puncture wound from the fight. It looked like a trip to the veterinarian for Frankie, a chore we always hated. It was almost impossible to get him into a pet carrying case. First he would fuss, meow, and then stretch himself out. Finally, we would roll him up like a ball and shove him into the carrying case. Even after getting him into the case, he fought and screamed like Siamese cats do all the way to the vet's hospital.

The veterinarian cleaned out the puncture wound under his eye and stitched it up. He gave us some salve to rub on it everyday until it healed. Going home, Frankie was a lot quieter. It was probably the medicine the vet gave him to calm him down.

I am not sure who won that fight, but we never saw the black cat again. Frankie now had his first scar, one of many he would get in the years to come. He was skinny, but very strong and fast. When his long tail would fluff up like a bottlebrush, he looked a lot bigger than he actually was. Well, at least, Frankie thought so!

Every cat that tried to come through the back yard eventually had to fight Frankie. Word spread throughout the Kingdom -- stay away from the Realm of Frankie, the King of Siam. Soon, we rarely saw any cats, except for an occasional one passing by through the field in the back. Always when any strange cat was passing by outside the fence, they would keep a great distance from Frankie's territory, never crossing over to this side of the fence. When one dared to come close, we could see Frankie crouched real low in the grass or behind a bush, staring at the passing intruder until it was out of sight.

Patroliing the fence line below

CHAPTER SIX

VISITORS WELCOME?

Frankie showed his protective nature not only with creatures passing through the yard, but also with any animal which might be with a friend who came to visit. Now, this might sound strange, but we had to be careful that friends and relatives didn't bring any pets with them when visiting. When we tried to explain to them that Frankie was not friendly to other animals, they thought we had a tiger as a pet.

One day, Mark, Charlie's friend, came unannounced and brought his new dog to show him off. Before we could stop him, he let his dog loose in the house. The dog probably caught Frankie's or Chico's scent and started down the hall sniffing. Mark began telling us how his new dog, a mixed breed, was the best guard dog you could ever have. I thought to myself, I better find Frankie and lock him into one of the bedrooms. I was concerned this guard dog might spot and attack

Frankie, but it was too late. While Mark's guard dog was sniffing down the hall, passing the door to one of the bedrooms, it happened! The dog started yelping and running down the hall towards us. What a scene! He was heading for the front door with Frankie on his back, riding him like a jockey and swatting him with both paws. As they passed, I grabbed Frankie and pulled him off the guard dog at the same time Charlie opened the front door. The guard dog bolted outside, yelping as it ran down the street with Mark now running after his dog, yelling, "What happened to my dog?!"

At the bottom of the street Mark finally caught his dog and brought it back to his car and locked it inside. He looked up at us and asked, "What happened?" We all were in tears, laughing so hard, trying to explain what had happened. We tried to explain that this was a common maneuver for Frankie. When someone would walk down the hall past a bedroom, it was one of Frankie's favorite games, jumping out and swatting you on the leg. It was a game he played, meant to scare you more than hurt you. In the guard dog's case, he jumped on his back and swatted him. That was a new game. I am sure the dog did not think it was a game nor a funny one, at that.

Frankie carrying a bunny rabbit

CHAPTER SEVEN

THE RABBIT HUNTER

The bunny incident happened on the same day as Charlotte and the children were preparing to leave on a trip to Hawaii. I could not take time off work and stayed home to watch and feed the animals.

While they were all packing and loading the luggage into the car, I noticed Frankie walking towards the house with a large fuzzy thing in his mouth. How cute, I thought. He is coming to the door to give Charlotte a going away gift. It looked like a big gopher, as he dropped it on the floor in front of us. We couldn't believe our eyes! It was a very small baby bunny. I picked up the fuzzy little animal, so small it could fit in the palm of my hand. We all looked at each other and thought, What do we do now with a small live bunny?

I went out in the backyard to the back fence line, thinking maybe I could find the place where the mother or other bunnies might be hiding. I didn't find any signs of other bunnies. I wish Frankie could tell us where he found this little thing. What are we going to do with the bunny? Charlotte came up with the idea to drop the bunny off at the Wildlife Center where they care for injured and orphaned animals. Perfect. They would drop off the bunny on the way to the airport. The family said goodbye and left, carrying the bunny.

After the family drove off, Frankie spent the better part of the hour looking in and around the house for the bunny, meowing all the time. It was a little like the old days when he used to retrieve the rabbit's foot, only this time, it was a whole rabbit.

Time flew by and the family returned from Hawaii. The animals and I were happy to see them back. Chico ran around barking and Frankie let out a couple of his loud meows.

No more bunnies had turned up or brought to the house by Frankie. Still, to this day, we do not know where Frankie found his bunny.

Frankie carrying snake in his mouth and snake wrapped around him, looking like he had 2 tails in back.

CHAPTER EIGHT

IT'S A ZEBRA! NO, A CAT WITH TWO TAILS! NO, FRANKIE WITH A SNAKE!

The summer was over and it was time for the traditional Labor Day barbeque. It had always been a great party. Lots of friends and family members came; there were at least 30 people attending the barbeque. All the children were in the swimming pool having a great time, while the adults were all gathered around the barbeque socializing. Chico was standing by the barbeque in hopes that maybe somebody would offer him a tidbit. Frankie was out in the back bushes, stalking and hunting like a leopard in Africa.

I yelled out, "Barbeque is done! Everyone grab a plate! It's time to eat!" After everyone had settled down and began to eat, one of the guests brought to our attention that out by the back fence they saw some kind of small animal come out of the bushes. Someone else remarked they could see it, but didn't know what it was. They said the animal had black stripes like a zebra with two tails.That made everyone laugh. The jokes continued. A guest remarked, "No, don't be silly, it is too small to be a zebra, but it does have stripes from head to tail." As the strange animal reached the back lawn next to the pool, we could see it was only Frankie with his tail wrapped around his body. I said "No, it can't be his tail. His tail is long, but not that long, and besides, it looks like he has two tails." Then Cori yells out, "It's Frankie with a black snake wrapped around him!" As he kept coming closer everyone began yelling to stop him before he brings the snake into the house. When Frankie jumped up on the deck and was heading for the kitchen, someone yelled," Do something!" The group of guests who were gathered on the deck scattered. Everyone panicked as they scrambled through the kitchen door into the house. Chico let out a slight bark and fled the scene, too! I put on my leather gardening gloves and approached Frankie who was on the deck with the snake still in his mouth. I did not know who had a hold on who. Frankie was gripping the snake by the head and the snake was wrapped all around Frankie's body. As I grabbed the snake, Frankie and the snake let go of each other at the same time. I took the snake to the back fence and turned it loose on the other side, in the grassy field. Someone else had grabbed Frankie. He was making a real fuss with loud meows. Roaring like a lion, he was put in a bedroom and the door shut. Minutes passed and we could still hear Frankie's loud meowing; he was not going to stop while locked in the bedroom. Finally, we couldn't stand the noise and had to let him back outside. He gets so mad when you take away any little creature he brings home as a trophy.

Kidnapping Frankie

A Masked man sneaking away carrying sack over shoulder with Frankie's head sticking out of bag.

CHAPTER NINE

THE KING HAS BEEN KIDNAPED

One day we couldn't find Frankie. Usually out hunting or just lurking in the grass watching his territory, he would come home when it was time for supper. We gave it little thought. When night had fallen, we were becoming concerned so I decided to get into my truck and drive around the neighborhood to look for him. After about half an hour of looking around and finding no sign of him, it was getting too dark so we decided to stop and wait until the next day to continue searching for him. Hopefully, he had not been hit by a car and lying injured by the side of the road somewhere.

Early the next morning, still no one had called about seeing Frankie. It was time to put out posters, contact the Humane Society, and let everyone in the neighborhood know that Frankie was missing. The flyers were posted on all poles within two miles of our house. We called the Humane Society asking if any cats had been turned in or were picked up. We drove all around, up and down all the streets in the neighborhood calling out his name. After a couple of days and no sign of Frankie, we thought maybe he was kidnapped and we would never see him again. Why would anyone kidnap Frankie the King when he wasn't even a real king. Yes, he was a beautiful cat with his blue eyes, shiny coat, and long tail, but he would never stand still and would be a terror if kept in a strange house. We were pretty certain of that. All we could do was wait and see if a neighbor called saying they had seen Frankie wandering around their area, or maybe he would finally find his way back home.

When Charlotte left for the private school she worked at, which was about a mile or so from our house, she posted another flyer at the gated entrance. Upon arrival at her job, she began telling everyone about the missing King. She told the night watchman who was getting off work after his night shift and all the teachers who were just arriving,

A week had passed and there was still no sign of Frankie. The Kingdom was in a total state of chaos. There was no one to patrol the fence line. Already we could see stray cats coming close to the fence. At night, raccoons were in our yard, sniffing around.

One morning, Charlotte decided to leave a little early for work and look around the school grounds. On her way she spotted the night watchman parked at the ruins of an old mansion by the gates to the school. She stopped her car right next to his. Greeting him, she asked, "Hi Joe, Frankie has still not come home. Have you seen any cats around?" "No," he said, "Hhowever, I did see something strange last night just before the sun came up. I saw a kind of weasel-looking thing. The animal ran across the road and into that large field of high grass over there." "What did it look like? What color was it?" Charlotte asked. He answered, "It was still a little dark so I couldn't see very clearly, but it was skinny, kind of brown, and had a long tail." Charlotte got really excited and thanked Joe as she drove off quickly. As soon as she got to work she called to tell me what the night watchman had said about the strange animal he had seen. It sounded like it could be Frankie, but then again it was a long way from home. My mind was racing with countless thoughts. He would not wander that far. It did not sound right that he would be just one or two miles from home, been gone for over a week, and couldn't find his way back home. He would not wander that far away and not be able to find his way home. If someone had found him, he had his collar on with his name and phone number. The only conclusion is that someone must have catnapped him.

The cat thief probably could not stand his loud yelling, so he dumped him off at the school grounds.

Jumping in my truck, I drove down to the old mansion where the night watchman had seen the strange weasel-like animal. I parked and started walking around the parking area, calling for Frankie as I searched around the grassy edges. Suddenly I heard this loud meowing coming from the field of high grass across the road. I ran across the road and into the field yelling out his name. He began his loud meowing noise and at the same time he was jumping high above the grass, high enough to see me! Frankie spotted me and we both ran towards each other until he jumped into my arms! What a glorious reunion this was! I rushed back to the truck, put him in the seat next to me and drove home. All the way home, he was making his loud familiar meow.

Other than his collar being gone, he was in pretty good shape and he had no injuries. It even rained a couple of days while he was missing, yet he looked just as shiny and smooth as when he disappeared. For sure, he had been living in some house; all the neighbors knew him and where he lived, so for sure it was not in this area. After being dumped, he must have been trying to find his way back home and to his Kingdom. I put food and water down and he did not hesitate a moment. Boy, was he hungry! Whoever had him didn't know Frankie ate only canned food and no kibble, or maybe the cat-nappers never fed him. After he finished eating, I gave him a new white sock to chew on. He was a very happy kitty now!

Frankie jumping high above the grass.

CHAPTER TEN

THE PEACEFUL KINGDOM

After many years of hunting, patrolling, and fighting, Frankie was beginning to mellow down. He loved to curl up where it was warm, out in the sun in the summer and beside the fireplace in the winter. He became a real buddy to every family dog we had, and even slept on the couch or bed with them.

There were lots of birds in the garden, along with the many lizards sunning out in the open. No one seemed to worry about the King and he did not bother them anymore. The Kingdom was in harmony now, a beautiful place with all the creatures under Frankie's rule living a very peaceful life.

Long Live the King!

The End

10620 Treena Street, Suite 230
San Diego, California,
CA 92131 USA
www.readersmagnet.com
1.619.354.2643
Copyright 2021 All Rights Reserved

www.ingramcontent.com/pod-product-compliance
Ingram Content Group UK Ltd.
Pitfield, Milton Keynes, MK11 3LW, UK
UKHW062001290726
14090UKWH00021B/1329

9 781955 603386